I0537467

Are Questions that Bad?

Hannah Rappaport

Owl King Publishing, LLC   Orange, CT

Are Questions that Bad?

Library of Congress Control Number: 2011901410

First Owl King Publishing Edition: February 2011

Printed in the United States of America

Dedicated To...

Everyone who has helped me in my life, to write and be happy...

My dad, who has been quite a role model in the writing world

My mom, who has been so kind to me and has taught me so much about poetry

My friends and family who have been so supportive of this book

All of my hermit crabs, who have taught me responsibility and kindness - Dizzy, who I have right now, and I really miss you, Racer, Tondue, Frisky, Surprise, Cupcake, Berry, and most of all,
Tiger

My teachers who have been so uplifting and have taught me all of the writing techniques I used for this book, especially Miss Greenspan, who hasn't just pushed me far in my writing, but has showed me who a good person really is and what they do. You also always answered my questions!

Mr. Licsak, who always complimented my writing especially in my PSA, and has also been an amazing LEAP teacher...I'll miss you!

Thank You!

Are Questions that Bad?

Contents

Chapter 1
The Flashback

Dear Diary,

I'm going to be your new owner. Since there's no one else for this job, I've chosen you to listen to my feelings and comfort me- you'll do that, right? Just so you know, my name is Lydia and before you start listening to my problems, I'd like you to know a few things about me:

1. I'm a vegetarian, and I don't know why people think it's so weird, but you don't...right?

2. This is a silly one, but I have to leave for the bus in a few minutes, so I can't tell

you too much. I'm in the fifth grade, and I go to Appleton Elementary School.

3. I like asking lots of questions. You'll probably realize this very soon. Here are some of the ones I want answered the most: "Why do my friends hate me, why doesn't anyone listen to me, why doesn't orange rhyme with anything, and most of all, why is it that whenever I ask anyone a question, their answer is either "I don't know", or "no". The latter is usually more common. To encourage us to ask questions, my teacher always says that even Albert Einstein was inquisitive, but there's one problem...he was a famous genius, so I bet he could figure out all of his problems by himself!

Anyway, I'd tell you more, but the bus is here, and I don't have time. I've had fun talking with you, and I have a hunch that even though you're a book, you're going to be one of the best friends I've ever had.

Yours truly,

Lydia Lips

Lydia threw the little diary onto the edge of her bed and scooped her backpack onto her shoulder, hurrying to the bus with an unusual smile on her face. Earlier, she'd met a new friend, not an actual person that you can play games with or call up on the phone to talk for hours, but a little book that listens just as much as any good friend could. Her mom had gotten it before she went on her business trip to Amsterdam. She told Lydia that she didn't want her to feel left alone while she was away in another country. Although Lydia had just stared at it for a couple weeks, this morning she had opened it up and was jubilant once she did. A friend, even one in the form of a book, was surely what she needed right now.

As the door of the bus opened, Lydia knew she wouldn't be saved a seat. She was used to it. Ever since she'd become a vegetarian, her best friend, Judy, was very mad at her for some reason. Lydia only had a faint idea of why...

The night after Lydia had decided to become a vegetarian, she was having an awesome sleepover with Judy. They played games, made friendship bracelets, and had a snack, all good stuff until Judy's mom called the girls in for dinner. Giggling, the girls ran to the table and hopped onto the mahogany wooden chairs. Judy smacked her lips at the sight of her favorite food, but Lydia had a distressed look on her face...the kind of look you get when you need to go to the bathroom, while on a road trip to Nebraska, and your mom announces that you're almost a quarter of the way there, even though you've been in the car for hours, and you could've sworn that you were going in circles.

Judy's mom glimpsed Lydia's face and smiled. "Don't worry; the food will cool down soon!"

Lydia sighed. It wasn't about that. There was a big hunk of meatloaf on her plate. As Judy wolfed it down, Lydia poked the brown lump with her fork and shuddered, wondering what animal had died for it. She'd become a vegetarian for her love of animals, and she wasn't about to start eating one now!

So, Lydia, with her love for asking questions, asked, "Um, do you have anything I could eat without meat in it?"

"What do you mean?" Judy asked in between mouthfuls of meatloaf. "This is my mom's special meatloaf. I thought you liked it, Lydia."

"Well, you see," Lydia didn't quite know how to put it, so she just blurted out the facts. "Yesterday, I decided to become a vegetarian, so I don't eat meat- I can't eat this meatloaf because it obviously has meat in it, hence the name-I was hoping you had some meatless food for me."

Lydia gasped for air having said all of that in one breath.

She expected Judy's mom to smile and in her mellow voice, say, "Oh, thanks for telling me Lydia, I had no idea you were a vegetarian, otherwise I would've made something else. Here, let me get you some peanut butter and jelly!" She'd stroll to the fridge, and make her the sandwich. Judy would blurt out, "Cool! I want to be a vegetarian, too!" And they would all eat dinner together happily and continue on with the sleepover.

Instead, Judy and her mom just sat there with the same distressed expression on their faces, just a bit more intense, like they were almost a quarter of the way to Japan. Judy's face soon became very angry.

"You just said that because you hate my mom's cooking, and you don't want to be my friend anymore!" she yelled. "Being vegetarian was a stupid excuse, anyway."

Lydia was shocked. She had no intention of it coming across that way. She just said that she was a vegetarian because she <u>was </u>a vegetarian! So, there she was, sitting at a dinner table with two things staring at her...a hunk of meatloaf and a girl who had totally misunderstood what she was saying, now sending knives across the room with her eyes-eyes that had just shone brightly with laughter but now froze over with ice.

Lydia broke the silence with another question, one that was probably the best thing anyone could say to break up a stuffy situation: "Do you think it would be good if you called my mom to pick me up now?"

"That might be good, Lydia," Judy's mom said quietly, getting up from her seat and nearing the phone.

Lydia poked at the meatloaf a couple of times, her eyes fixed on her shoes below the table. She wouldn't dare look Judy's way across the table as her mother dialed the Lips' number. She frowned as she listened to their conversation with her eyes still fixed on the floor.

"Hello, Karen, can you pick Lydia up from our house now ... no, she didn't get sick on the floor ... no, Lydia didn't get hurt ... it was just a minor situation ... thank you! Bye."

Until her mom came, Lydia pretended that all of this would blow over, and when she walked into the classroom on Monday, Judy would smile, and then run over to her, laughing, and...

"Lydia, your mom's here," announced Judy's mom, smothering Lydia's high hopes of what Monday would bring.

As she got up from her seat, Lydia dared one last look at Judy. She gave one final smile across the table in her friend's direction, trying to make her best, "I'm-so-sorry-can-we-still-be-friends?" face.

Judy wasn't looking back, because she was bringing up her dishes, the meatloaf cleaned right off, with her back turned to the table.

Lydia sighed, and under her breath she muttered, "Bye". She could just faintly see Judy rolling her eyes.

She got into the car, looking longingly out the window all the way home. Her mom didn't ask any questions about what had made the sleepover end before anyone was even thinking about sleeping.

She just placed a small purple book with a lace bow in the middle on Lydia's lap and said softly, "This is for you while I'm gone, in case you need someone to talk to while I'm in Amsterdam."

Lydia threw the book aside. All she wanted to talk to right now was Judy. She also wanted to ask questions, but she didn't know who to ask. Nobody would answer her, anyway.

She asked herself the same question again and again the car ride home: "Why was being a vegetarian who asked lots of questions so bad?"

Just thinking about her horrible fight with Judy made Lydia frown. As she walked onto the bus she could probably guess who Judy was saving a seat for-Bess.

Lydia wasn't sure who Bess was, but she must be Judy's new best friend. They'd done everything together since Lydia and Judy's fight. Lydia's high hopes for Monday had been squashed, but as she walked into school on that sad day, she thought about something: her question had ruined a whole friendship. Imagine, are questions that bad?

Chapter 2
Ghouls, Goblins, and Lydia

Dear Diary,

Today is Halloween, and I'm so excited! But one thing I'm not excited about is that this is the first Halloween in a long time I won't be spending with Judy. Yesterday, I was thinking about the fight we had that made us break up. You'd probably listen to it, but I don't feel like talking about it. She used to be my best friend, but now she doesn't even save me a seat on the bus. I think it's all because I became a vegetarian. Is being vegetarian really that bad? Oh, there I go asking questions again! But, really, is it that bad? I did it because I love animals and my dad is allergic to fur and feathers. That meant that I couldn't have many kinds of pets. He offered that I could have a pet turtle, but I'm not really a turtle type, and since turtles aren't domesticated, I don't think it's humane to keep them as pets. You'd do the same thing, right? Although, if I *did* have a pet, it would listen to me...or maybe it would hate me like everyone else does. I think I can only rely on you, Dear Diary.

Yours truly,

Lydia Lips

"Dad, please, I can do it myself!" grumbled Lydia, pulling her dad's hand away from her sleeve. "Putting on a costume isn't that hard!"

"I'm sorry Lyd, it's just because your mom can't assist you with your costume this year, I thought you might have needed a little help," Lydia's dad coaxed.

He was right; Lydia's mom had made her awesome Halloween costumes ever since she was born: pretty princesses, wicked witches, and vivid vampires. Last year, she won the costume contest at her school, but now, since her mom was on an important business trip to Amsterdam, from the beginning of October, until Thanksgiving, she couldn't make her a costume.

Lydia's mom was a saleswoman at Flavor Toys, which is probably the best job a kid's parent could have, considering you get to try out all of the new toys they make! A company in The Netherlands with a Dutch name that Lydia couldn't pronounce wanted to sell their products with Flavor Toys to make a massive combined toy company, and Mrs. Lips needed to negotiate an agreement.

A year ago, when Lydia heard that her mom was going on this trip, she was overjoyed, because the company said her mom could bring the family along, but that all changed a month ago. They were packing for the trip, when a big client who was going to buy a whole load of toys decided to buy from a cheaper company. Flavor Toys lost a whole bunch of money, which prevented Mrs. Lips from bringing her whole family to Amsterdam with her.

Lydia was devastated at first, but then she realized that if she went, she'd be missing lots of school and most of all, trick or treating!

She hadn't realized, though, that she'd have no costume, because her mom hadn't made her one yet and wouldn't be sending any costumes from Europe!

Lydia had to face the facts-she'd have to make the costume herself this year. Of course, there were other options like buying the costume or letting her dad help her make it, but she was broke, and would never let her dad close to a thread and needle.

After sewing, pinning, and cutting, Lydia was pretty happy with her costume. She was going as a hobo, asking people to donate money to UNICEF. She took a stick from her backyard and tied a handkerchief around it. In there she placed the UNICEF box. She sewed a patchwork shirt, and wore an old, ripped pair of jeans. It was good she wasn't such a good seamstress, because the shirt looked even more like what a hobo might wear.

She struggled not to get poked by one of the bobby pins in her costume, and at the same time, swatted her dad away from helping her put it on. He could get annoying sometimes.

"Who are you trick or treating with?" he asked. "Judy, right?"

Lydia shrugged. She really didn't know.

Judy had always done everything with her ever since they were little. Lydia was hoping she'd see Judy trick or treating and beg for forgiveness. Then, they'd spend the rest of the night together. At least that's what she hoped would happen.

"Bye, Lyd," called Lydia's dad as she walked out the front door.

Lydia waved, ran to the neighbor's house, and rang the doorbell. They'd probably give her lots of money for UNICEF. An elderly lady lived there, and she'd always been a very nice neighbor.

"Trick or treat!" called Lydia. "I'm collecting money for UNICEF. Will you please give a few pennies for kids in need?"

The lady pursed her lips together, studying Lydia. "What are you, some movie actor that's famous these days? I don't really follow all of that. Now go, here's some candy."

She placed a bowl of Kit Kats in front of Lydia's face.

Lydia frowned. "I'm collecting money for UNICEF-not candy! Could you spare a penny, please?" she asked, getting a bit impatient now.

"What? You want money? I thought you kids wanted candy! Now you want money? Who changed the rules? Anyway, I don't have my purse here, so shoo! Shoo, you movie actor!" the lady yelled.

Lydia walked away. Maybe this woman wasn't as nice as she remembered. "Oh, and I'm a hobo!" Lydia shouted.

She walked to the next house, hoping she'd have more luck this time. She wasn't sure who lived there, but she had high hopes.

The door opened to a young woman with a smiling face.

"Trick or treat! I'm collecting money for UNICEF. Will you please give a few coins for kids in need?"

The woman kept grinning, holding out the bucket of candy.

"Uh, no, ma'am. I'm collecting money, not candy-for UNICEF, you know, the organization?" Lydia held out the box, waiting for money.

"Oh, I see. But wouldn't you rather have some candy? I don't have money ready right now. Go on, take a Twix!" she said, still smiling.

Lydia took a Twix as she was told, for she really had no other choice. She started to walk off.

"Oh, and nice movie actor costume," she heard, as she walked.

"I'm a hobo!!" Lydia yelled back. The door had already been closed.

Lydia had even higher hopes for the next house. Someone was <u>bound</u> to have heard of UNICEF and give her money. She was <u>only</u> asking for a few coins. This was the house across the street from Judy. She knocked on the door.

"Trick or treat! I'm collecting money for UNICEF. Will you please give a few pennies for kids in need?"

As she spoke, Lydia saw a big burly man looking down at her and shuffling his hand around in his pocket. Yes, finally a few coins!

Instead, he handed Lydia a twenty dollar bill and grinned under his moustache. "Go buy yourself something kid. Love the movie actor look!" he said in a very deep voice.

"Um, thank you, sir, but I'm not buying myself anything, this is for charity. And, are you sure you want to give me twenty dollars? I'm only asking for coins, oh, and I'm a hobo, not a movie actor!" Lydia said, amazed at this overly generous man.

"Charity, shmarity! Knock yourself out, kid!" The man closed the door.

Clutching the bill tightly, Lydia walked out with a puzzled look. She heard giggling from around the corner, took a flashlight out of her "hobo bag", and carefully clicked it on, shining it around the corner. Two girls emerged-one a witch and the other a scarecrow. Lydia could just make out their faces with the flashlight-Judy and Bess!

Ugh! Judy was already trick or treating with Bess after two months of not being friends with Lydia.

Lydia was really mad, but maybe her plan could still work. Maybe if she apologized, they could ditch Bess and still go trick or treating together.

"Judy!" called Lydia with an excited tone.

Judy looked down, frowning.

"Lydia, is that you? From school, right? I'm on your bus! Come trick or treat with us!" said Bess, grinning.

Lydia didn't know what else to do. She was hoping she could just trick or treat alone with Judy. At least this was a start to becoming friends again. She walked across the street to the two girls, smiling.

She noticed that Judy wasn't smiling back. She was gnawing on some taffy, looking casually in another direction.

"Judy, Lydia from school is trick or treating with us. That's okay, right?" asked Bess.

Judy just kept chewing and managed to make a "mmf" sound.

"I'll take that as a yes," said Bess.

Lydia could tell it wasn't.

"It's dark tonight, right?" asked Lydia, trying to break the awkwardness.

Bess just stared at her. "So, Lydia, have you gotten any good candy yet? Did you eat any?"

Lydia shook her head 'no'. "I'm trick or treating for UNICEF, so I'm asking for money instead of candy. Anyway, if I got any candy, I'd have to see if it's vegetarian before I eat it."

Judy suddenly stopped chewing and turned around. Without the flashlight, Lydia could tell she was frowning.

"Lydia, I know you eat candy, and I know you're not vegetarian. You're making this entire vegetarian thing up because I'm here! You were looking for us trick-or-treating just so you could be mean to me again! Lydia Lips, just go away!" yelled Judy.

"Lydia, is this right?" asked Bess, her hands on her hips.

Lydia was speechless. How could Judy think of her like this? She really was vegetarian! She wanted to apologize and have an awesome rest of the night trick or treating together, but Judy blew it.

Lydia walked home sadly and heard from Bess and Judy: "And we hate your movie actor costume!" Normally, Lydia would have asked another one of those questions. "Why does everyone think I'm a movie actor when I'm a hobo?" Instead, she just kept walking, her throat dry and hoarse. Her legs felt tired and weak. Her Halloween had been ruined. As she walked, she really did feel like a hobo, but instead of being homeless, she was friendless.

Chapter 3
The Tasting Game

Dear Diary,

It's November, and that means Judy's birthday is coming up. Last year, it was so much fun! I was the only person invited. I went to her house, where we watched a movie, gave ourselves makeovers, played with her dog, and swam in her indoor pool—I know, cool, right? Why don't I have an indoor pool? Actually, it's so much money; I don't even need to ask that question. Last year, Judy made such a fuss inviting me to her party. On the bus she told everyone about all the fun things that would be happening. She said everyone could come ... as long as their name was Lydia! I laughed, then she laughed, and then we both were laughing. How come it seems like I haven't laughed in years? Diary, will you tell me a joke? Wait, never mind, no offense, but I just remembered you're a book. Books are good, you can read them and write in them, but you can't go to their house; they don't have one, unless their cover counts as a house. You can't give them makeovers; they don't have faces, unless you count the front of them. I suppose you can watch movies with them, but it wouldn't be the same, and they definitely don't have a dog or an indoor pool. I'm sorry, Diary, if it seems like I'm being mean. I really do appreciate you. I'm just very worried that I won't be invited to Judy's birthday party this year. Actually, I'm almost positive I won't. I bet Bess doesn't even know when Judy's birthday is! It's November 12th by the way! Maybe I can celebrate your birthday on that horrible day instead.

Yours truly,
    Lydia Lips

Once again, Lydia neared the bus, knowing she wouldn't be saved a seat. She pictured Judy and Bess sitting together and laughing, much like she and Judy used to do.

It was a crisp fall morning, as most days in the beginning of November were. The sun shone, and there was a breeze, as rainbows of leaves crunched under her feet on her way up the steps to the door of the bus. This was no ordinary autumn breeze that drifts by in a slow, warm, way. It was more of a winter breeze.

There is a big distinction: fall breezes send warmth and good vibes, but winter breezes are the opposite. Lydia wondered what could be so bad coming, as she walked through the bus door.

Instead of Judy and Bess sitting next to each other, giggling, Judy was standing up and babbling about something. Lydia walked down the aisle.

"As many of you know," said Judy, "my birthday's coming up and so is my party! My party is the best one around and most of you will want to come. We'll watch movies, play games, and most of all, swim in my fabulous indoor pool. Best of all, we'll have it all to ourselves! Did I mention the water slide?"

Judy went on and on about her party. In various seats, oohs and aahs could be heard.

Lydia could imagine what Judy was going to say next. "And everyone can come! If your name is Bess, that is!"

She actually said something very different: "You can come if you win the Tasting Game!"

"What in the world is that?" thought Lydia.

Judy dug into two large paper bags on the floor of the bus in front of her seat. Her hand emerged with a spoon and a jar covered in paper, hiding the contents.

"You're first, Kit!" said Judy, moving to the back of the bus. "Close your eyes and guess what food I'm putting in your mouth!"

Kit, being the nervous and quiet person she was, put her hand over her eyes as Judy placed the spoon into the jar.

"Open up!" said Judy.

Kit opened her mouth, the spoon went in, and a puzzled look came across her face. "Is it pizza with peaches on it?" she asked quietly.

As Kit swallowed, Judy shouted, "Wrong! Next, Bill will try to guess the same food!"

Judy got a new spoon out of her bag and strolled to Bill, one seat forward on the bus, with the same covered jar. They went through the same steps and Bill guessed, "Ice cream with apples and spaghetti?"

"No!" yelled Judy. "Lola's next!"

Judy kept going through the bus yelling, "Wrong! Wrong! Wrong!"

Lydia wondered what the food could possibly be with answers all over the place like: "Beans with a hint of jelly?" or "Strawberries and peanut butter!"

Finally, Judy got to Bess and took a new spoon, scooped it in the jar, and made Bess close her eyes to guess the food.

The spoon went slowly through her open lips, and Bess licked the mysterious food clean off with her tongue. She made a few smacking noises before she finally swallowed. After swallowing, she opened her eyes and licked her lips once more.

Judy's hands slid to her hips, her foot tapping on the floor, before Bess finally opened her mouth again.

"I'm not positive, but could that food possibly be mashed up cucumber and salsa with a pinch of oregano and cinnamon?" she said.

"Correct!" shouted Judy. "I guess you'll be the only one coming to my party!"

She said that with a smirk on her face, as if the whole thing had been planned. And Lydia hadn't even had a turn. That sure wasn't fair!

"Wait a minute," said Lydia. "I didn't get a turn; you said everyone could have a try!"

Judy sneered. "I didn't forget you! Let me get a new spoon and a jar with a different food in it."

Something about that sneer made Lydia quiver, but if she guessed the food correctly, she could go to Judy's party and apologize to her.

Judy lifted another jar out of her paper bag, and got out another spoon. She walked to the front of the bus where Lydia sat, and motioned for her to close her eyes. Lydia slowly opened her mouth, waiting for a spoon with some weird substance on it to pass her lips.

"Yuck! Bacon with pickle! OMG! I ate bacon!" screamed Lydia, hopping out of her seat and starting to cry.

Even if it meant having to wait even longer to apologize to Judy, Lydia truly hoped she'd guessed wrong. She had never intended to eat any animal again and she blew it!

"Darn," muttered Judy. "You're right. You can come to my party, but stop playing the stupid joke that you're a vegetarian. It's really mean, and nobody thinks it's funny."

Although Lydia had won, she wasn't too excited. At least now she could get her friendship back at the party.

Lydia walked off the bus to the school building. Actually, she wasn't happy at all.

Chapter 4
Once Again in the Indoor Pool

Dear Diary,

Today is November 12, and you remember that day, right? It's Judy's birthday. I was invited to her party, and you must think I'm happy about that. Well, I'm not! She tricked me into eating bacon to prove that I'm not a vegetarian, but I am! You know that, right diary? She didn't even have any intention of inviting me. She just wanted to trick me and have the party with Bess! The only good part about going to the party is the indoor pool-oh, and it would be the perfect place to apologize to her to get our friendship back. But if I don't, I'll still have you as a friend. Is it really worth having a friend who tricked you? I suppose it's better than not having a friend at all. See you after the party!

Yours truly,

Lydia Lips

"Bye, Lyd! Have fun with your friends!" called Lydia's dad as she got out of the car and started to make her way over to the front door of Judy's house for the party.

That was the thing, they weren't friends. Just a couple of weeks ago on Halloween, Judy and Bess had been quite mean to her, all because they thought she wasn't telling the truth about being vegetarian. It really <u>was</u> a stupid quarrel they had gotten themselves into.

Lydia had only been allowed the chance to go to this party because of her extremely good taste buds, and she was happy about that-sort of. She had eaten bacon, but now she might be able to get a friend back.

But right now, they still weren't friends ... yet. An apology goes a long way you know, and that's why having eaten bacon didn't seem so bad at the moment. It was a one way ticket to Getting Your BFF Back Land. Now to board the train!

"Ding-Dong," sounded Judy's doorbell. Lydia had rung it thousands of times before for countless play dates, but this time, her stomach lurched as if she'd never rung <u>any</u> doorbell before.

Judy's mom opened the door. She grinned at Lydia as if she could sense the girls' fight had been resolved.

"Come right in Lydia. The girls are in the backyard," said Judy's mom.

Lydia walked through the house to the back door without needing any assistance. She had done this thousands of times before, too.

Judy's backyard always seemed to be gorgeous. Sometimes the grass in Lydia's yard was trampled or brown, but Judy's was always a lush shade of green. That's because her dad's a professional gardener. He designs what people's plants in their yard should look like and then plants them. Usually the woman is the one in the household with the green thumb!

That's also the reason they had an indoor pool, not because they're rich or something, but because someone very rich was her dad's customer one time. She was so ecstatic about the array of orchids he planted in her front yard that instead of paying him in money, she paid by having an indoor pool installed in the Copal's house.

Lydia remembered that day as if it were yesterday, but it was actually a couple of years ago. The pool had been installed, and the girls already had their swimsuits on the night before, waiting for the moment to splash into the gaping hole filled with water.

They held hands and jumped in together, smiling underwater and making bubbles as they laughed. When they came up, they gasped for air and vowed that they'd always be friends.

Lydia sighed as she walked past the pool room to the back door. She needed to reclaim that vow.

Opening the back door, Lydia could see that Judy and Bess were popping brightly-colored balloons in the cool autumn wind. They froze, not making one more loud pop, almost like someone had shot them with a tranquilizer gun, as the door creaked open.

"Hi guys! I'm here!" shouted Lydia, trying to sound enthusiastic.

Judy and Bess glanced at each other awkwardly, their mouths glued shut.

Finally, Bess managed to mutter, "Yeah, hi."

Judy hoisted a balloon, ready to pop it and go on with the party. "You should be very happy that you get to be at a fun party like this," she said, still holding the rubbery yellow balloon. "Now go put on a bathing suit and don't ruin our fun!"

Lydia nodded and went back into the house to do as she was told. She wasn't going to ruin the fun, she was going to enhance it (but also use it to get a friendship back).

When she was finally in the bathroom, she reached into her tote bag and pulled out her polka-dotted, pink tankini, thinking.

Putting on the swim top, she went over her plan of apology one more time: she'd swim underwater in the indoor pool and poke Judy, getting her attention. Then, she'd take a breath of air and apologize, making sure Judy knew that she was a vegetarian for her love of animals, never meaning to offend her. Finally, they'd have an awesome rest of the party.

"Bang!" The girls had popped the rest of the balloons. Lydia heard them entering the pool room as she left the bathroom.

Following them into the baby blue room, Lydia was confident that her plan would work.

"Wow! This is amazing! You're so lucky!" gasped Bess, her short brown hair covered in a red Speedo swim cap and her braces glistening.

"No, you're the lucky one to be at this party!" said Judy, grinning. "Hop in!"

Everyone splashed in the pool, not saying a word for awhile but enjoying the heated water, a nice change from the cold outside.

Finally, Lydia sprang into action, diving underwater and poking Judy's leg.

"Ouch! What'd you do that for?!" yelled Judy, startling Bess, and making her splash water in surprise.

Lydia was about to make her comeback - apologize and get everything straight, but instead, she asked another one of those questions.

"Can you come to my house for Thanksgiving? Your mom can bring the meatloaf. I used to be a vegetarian for my love of animals, but to get our friendship back together, I decided to stop." That was a lie, a white lie with good intention. Plus, it had a good chance of paying off later.

"So, now that I can eat your mom's meatloaf, can you bring it?" Lydia lied again.

"Um, sure. I'm sorry for everything, Lydia, by the way. Do you want to be friends again?" asked Judy, holding her arm.

"Sure," said Lydia. Her plan had worked perfectly, even better, because Judy was the one apologizing.

The party went along very smoothly after that, with all of the girls friends again. Lydia just had a little business to do at the end.

Before her dad picked her up, Lydia went up to Mrs. Copal to whisper something in her ear, "On Thanksgiving, there will be a meatloaf on your doorstep. Take it in and pretend you made it. Bring it to my house for dinner!"

As she got into the car, Lydia felt overjoyed that her plan was working out. All she needed to do was make a tofu meatloaf, and everybody would be happy!

Chapter 5
A Trick with Good Intention and Tofu Turkey!

Dear Diary,

Today is Thanksgiving. I'm writing to you from the airport, to finally pick up my mom! I'm in the car right now, and I brought you because I thought I'd be really bored. I was right. There's a huge crowd, and I'm having a very hard time looking for my mom in it, so I'd like to talk to you about something...I got my friendship back with Judy! I had to lie for it, but that's not that bad, right? I had good intentions. I'm pretending that I stopped being vegetarian for her, and it worked! I made a tofu meatloaf last night, and I put it on the Copal's' doorstep. Mrs. Copal will pretend that she made it, and I'll eat it so Judy will be happy, making us friends again! Awesome plan, right? Wait a minute, I see golden brown hair, oh, and a grey suit with, yes!—the single rose pin I got my mom for her birthday! It's her! She's finally back from Amsterdam! I'm so excited! I really need to go now!

Yours truly,

Lydia Lips

Lydia bolted out of the car, very excited to see her mother in the massive crowd of strangers.

"Excuse me, pardon me," said Lydia as she swerved around aggravated ladies in dresses and puzzled men in suits, making her way to her mother.

"Mom!" yelled Lydia, jumping up and hugging her surprised mother by the waist.

"Lydia! You've grown so much!" cried Lydia's mom.

"Mom, it's only been a couple of months," said Lydia.

As the reunited mother and daughter strolled hand in hand to the car, Mrs. Lips made lots of small talk, such as, "How was Halloween, what were you for Halloween, how have you been doing in school, etc."

Lydia didn't mind, and she answered as best as she could. After all, she <u>was</u> with her mom again. Then Mrs. Lips asked another question.

"Have you written in the diary I gave you?"

"Maybe," said Lydia. Diaries are kind of embarrassing, and Lydia was thinking of getting rid of it since she had Judy to talk to now. It seemed kind of stupid talking to a book anyway.

"Well, that's too bad," said Lydia's mom.

All the way home, her mom blabbed on and on about the sights and adventures she saw and had on her business trip to Amsterdam. Lydia blocked out the conversation, and thought about how the vegetarian Thanksgiving approved by her dad at her house would go. She could see the sun setting through the back seat window of the car already, mad at Daylight Savings Time!

The family got home, changed into nice clothes, set the table, and got the house ready for their guests. Before the Copal family and her grandparents came, Lydia threw out the diary because she didn't need the little book anymore. Her plan was working perfectly without it.

"Ding, Dong!"

Her grandparents from her mom's side came in.

"Ding, Dong!"

Her grandparents from her dad's side came in.

"Ugh!" groaned Lydia as they pinched her cheeks, told her how much she'd grown, and offered her mints.

Finally, the doorbell rang one more time and Judy ran through the doorway, followed by her dad and then her mom, carrying a meatloaf! Lydia's plan was working!

The girls sat together at the table, once again the friends they used to be, laughing just for the sake of being together.

Mr. Lips started bringing in the main meal, a potluck of all different things: sweet potato and marshmallow fluff, cornbread, stuffing, cranberry sauce, and the meatloaf!

Judy opened her mouth to speak. "You know, I'm really sorry about the meatloaf thing," she said. "I'm glad you're eating it now, so let's dig in!"

As everyone started eating, the families went around the table telling what they were thankful for, and Judy and Lydia said it together... "Our friendship!" they exclaimed, laughing.

Finally, the turkey was brought out, and the lights dimmed. It wasn't actually a turkey. It was tofurkey (tofu turkey), because Lydia insisted they let turkeys give thanks, too, and her dad gave in. Nobody seemed to notice anyway. They were all too busy enjoying the night.

When it was time to leave, everyone hugged, and Lydia and Judy decided to schedule more play dates. Everything had gone how Lydia wanted: she and Judy were friends again, nobody found any difference with the meatloaf or the tofu turkey, and her mom had come back from Europe. Who could ask for anything more?!

Chapter 6
Busted!

Lydia lay down in her bed, thinking about how much she lucked out and how nothing could go wrong.

At the Copal's house that very minute, everyone was already up and eating breakfast. The whole family was sitting together, and Judy and Mr. Copal had contented faces as they ate their cereal. Mrs. Copal's face was very different. She looked distressed, similar to when Lydia had asked her question. This face was more secretive, because she <u>was</u> keeping a secret.

It strained her to take every bite, and her legs jiggled when she went to the refrigerator to get more orange juice. She was worried about the night before.

As everyone cleared their place settings, she hurried to dump out her trash, put her plate in the sink, and run out of the room. She didn't want to hurt anyone, but the secret brought her shoulders to a slump with all the weight of it.

Meanwhile, Lydia had been soaking up the happiness of success. She thought of all the things she and Judy could do like they used to, because they were friends again. They could stay up late, watching scary movies with popcorn, blankets, and her mom's homemade cookies. They could bask in Judy's indoor pool, playing "Marco, Polo" and seeing who could hold their breath the longest. They could have sleepovers, make skits, take funny photos, and give each other makeovers. They could do everything that anyone could possibly do together, especially without Bess or anyone else. Lydia lay on her bed with her eyes closed and her hands folded behind her head.

Mrs. Copal was biting things now. That's what she does when she's nervous. She bit her nails and her lip. She couldn't lie to her own daughter, but it would make her so angry if she found out. It would ruin her friendship with Lydia, but maybe Lydia was a bad friend to trick Judy. On the other hand, it could have been out of love, but how can you trick someone out of love? She was very confused.

Judy walked into her mom's room, breaking up her mother's confusion.

"Hey, mom?" she asked. "Can I invite Lydia over for dinner on Sunday? You can cook the meatloaf she really likes."

Her mom looked like she was a bomb about to go off, for she had no idea what to say, so she just blurted it out...

Lydia thought about inviting Judy over to her house at that moment. She wouldn't mind having an unplanned play date, since they <u>were</u> best friends again. Having a best friend is an experience everyone should have. Actually, it's more like a feat to accomplish, not just your average-day thing. Not everyone can find the right person for her, being interesting, funny, loyal, whatever suits her needs. Having a best friend is also a privilege. Not everyone has one or can even get one. Lucky for Lydia, she didn't need to worry about that. She already had the most perfect and wonderful best friend anyone could ever get.

She walked over to the phone, thinking about her awesome best friend, as she started to dial the number: (203) 555-9842, a number she'd be calling a lot now!

"I'm so sorry, Judy!" Mrs. Copal exclaimed. "That Lydia's an awful trickster, who I bet didn't even trick you out of love, because I don't even think that's possible!"

"Mom, what are you saying?!! Lydia's a nice girl, and I don't know how you think she tricked me! She wouldn't do that!" cried Judy, in disbelief. "You're wrong!"

"No, sweetheart, Lydia tricked you when you didn't realize it. You thought she was just being nice, but she wasn't," said Mrs. Copal with a sigh.

"No! No! Give me proof, tell me details, tell me when, tell me what, tell me everything!" yelled Judy.

"Remember Thanksgiving?" started Mrs. Copal.

"Of course!" said Judy. "Lydia was so kind and ate and loved your special meatloaf. I don't get your point!"

"That is the point," said Judy's mom. "It wasn't my special meatloaf, it was hers. She left it on our doorstep, and I think it was tofu."

"I don't believe it," said Judy. "Never in a million years, until I could breathe on Mars and eat pickles through a straw!"

"Believe it, honey. Her dad told me that he got tofu turkey especially for her," Mrs. Copal whispered.

From that point, Judy was a bawling mess. "We can never, ever be friends again!"

"Come here, sweetie," coaxed Mrs. Copal, hugging her daughter on her bed, sad that she had to be the messenger of such bad news.

They sat together on the bed for awhile, enjoying each other's comforting company, until the phone rang, making each of them jump.

Finally, Judy picked up, and Lydia got ready to joyfully ask her to come over.

"Hi, Judy!" she said enthusiastically.

There was a long pause, and Lydia could hear quiet sniffling through the receiver until Judy responded.

"Lydia, I hate you," Judy whispered.

Lydia was completely puzzled until Judy continued.

"You tricked me. You're a bad person. You're a liar. I wish we never were friends because you broke my heart, Lydia Lips. You broke it."

Lydia had no idea what to say. She could have asked what was wrong, but instead she got mad and asked another one of those bad, bad questions: "And like you didn't trick me?!"

There was another pause, but Judy stopped sniffling and talked again.

"Fine, I tricked you. We tricked each other. Good, now we're even and we can never be friends again."

"Good. I hate you too," said Lydia stormily. She hung up right there with a loud bang and hopped onto her bed. A friendship based on trickery can't be a good one, but she really wanted a friend just the same. Just a minute ago, they had been best friends. Maybe the second "F" of BFF hadn't worked out.

Lydia started to cry when she thought of all the fun she had had with Judy over the years. She slid to the floor, slowly, and sifted her hand around in her trash can for something. Finally, she pulled out the scruffy diary from her mother that she'd thrown out just a day before. She'd need it again.

Chapter 7
Shop till You Drop

Dear Diary,

I'm really sorry I threw you out. I thought I didn't need you anymore, but I was wrong and I'm really sorry about it. I thought I was friends with Judy, but I'm not. I thought everything was okay, but it isn't. I'm back without any friends but you, no offense, but I still miss Judy. She said our tricks could cancel each other out, so we must be even again, right? Now she'll just be doing everything with Bess and I'll have no one. I said I hated her and I'm not sure if I meant it. But one thing I'm sure about is that when I go shopping for holiday gifts, I am not buying Judy anything anymore. We were going to buy each other friendship bracelets, but now we aren't. Now we're not even shopping together, and I hope I don't bump into her at the store. I don't want to see her ever again!! Wait, my mom's calling me to leave now. Maybe I'll buy you a sticker for your cover.

Yours truly,
  Lydia Lips

Lydia and her mom set off to go holiday shopping. They always needed to buy a lot of presents, because their whole family exchanged gifts with one another.

Although she hated shopping, Lydia thought that it could take her mind off her and Judy's fight just minutes before. But Lydia had no idea that she was shopping on the worst shopping day of the year: Black Friday.

Mrs. Lips had asked her to come along because she didn't want to go shopping alone. She said that it would have been too much trouble and that Lydia knew what her whole family wanted.

They had a big family. The Lips would always invite their cousins, relatives, and friends over for a big holiday feast and celebration, and with that, came gifts. So many gifts that if the stack fell over, it would squish an average-sized human being.

All through the car ride, Lydia was quiet, thinking about her fight that was not so long ago. Mrs. Lips had no idea about it. What would she think about her daughter not having any friends? And even more, what would Lydia think about not having any friends? So far, she didn't like it.

They finally came to the Clifton Mall, a short drive from their home in the middle of town.

Walking to the entrance, they huddled together, not just trying to warm themselves in the autumn air, but also trying not to get trampled by all of the people pouring in.

Squeezing through the door cramped with shoppers, Lydia and her mom entered Toys Galore, a rival of Flavor Toys, but Mrs. Lips said she'd feel too silly shopping in her own work place on her day off.

"Now, let's start shopping for your little cousins. You have four, right? Yeah, they're coming over. Five, six, seven, and eight are their ages, right?" asked Mrs. Lips. She asked lots of questions when she was overwhelmed.

"Yeah, Mom - Lucy, Joseph, Hailey, and Mimi," answered Lydia. "Let's get them all matching Blanket Pets. That'll be really cute!"

They walked past the baby aisle, the toddler aisle, and finally got to the children 4-8 aisle. It was crammed with busy shoppers, all looking for the perfect gift for their child. Most were crowded around the new Blanket Pets that were just put in the store for holiday shopping.

"My Alice wants a pig Blanket Pet and if she doesn't get it she'll have a tantrum!" yelled a lady a few feet away, fighting an old man for the blanket.

"Well, my grandson Jimmy wants that pig so much that if he doesn't get it I'll sue!" he shouted, tugging at the pink blanket with fluffy pig head and feet sticking out.

Lydia tugged at her mother's sleeve, uncomfortably. "Mom, ask them to give us four Blanket Pets so we can just leave this store! Say that they're blocking the shelf with their tug of war over the pig." Lydia whispered into her mom's ear.

"Er, excuse me," muttered Mrs. Lips, trying to get the attention of the two fighting adults.

"Go away! You can't have my pig!" yelled the woman, almost snarling.

"No, we just want four *other* Blanket Pets for our little cousins."

"No, these are all mine!" shouted the man, almost growling, as he resumed tugging the blanket away from the nasty woman.

Mrs. Lips sighed. "Do you want to go clothes shopping? We can just get everyone a sweater there, and it might not be as crowded," she said.

"Sure," responded Lydia, walking with her mom to the escalator and along the way seeing many more silly fights over action figures, video games, and stuffed animals.

"Whirr, whirr, whirr." Lydia always loved going on the escalator. It was like an amusement park ride, for free, to go somewhere new.

She stepped off, catching her balance and smiling when she saw that the department store wasn't as crowded as Toys Galore. In fact, it wasn't crowded at all!

First, they went to the women's section to get a sweater for Mrs. Lips's sister. There was a gorgeous light pink one on a hidden rack behind the pants. It looked like they could actually snatch it without getting in one of those gift fights.

Lydia ran up to the rack, but just as she was about to pull the sweater off, a woman popped out from behind a pair of pants, making Lydia stir with fright.

"<u>My</u> sweater! Everything in this store is <u>mine</u>! You shall not take it!" she shouted at Lydia.

So that was why the store wasn't crowded. Lydia still couldn't believe how people changed so much when they wanted to buy a present. She wanted to get a present, too-especially one for her Uncle Mort. He was her favorite relative because at family gatherings, he was the only one to pay attention to her. Everyone else stopped to say how much she'd grown. Then they'd just mingle and blab the night away, but Uncle Mort would actually talk to Lydia, tell jokes, and be kind to her. If he wasn't there, she'd just have to play with her little cousins!

"Can we get a present for Uncle Mort?" Lydia asked as they walked out of the store to get away from the mean lady.

"Sure, Lydia. Let's hope we can get our hands on one. Black Friday is crazy," answered Mrs. Lips.

"What's Black Friday?" asked Lydia, anxious to know what made people so mad as to fight with each other over blankets.

"A day I now know not to go shopping," replied Lydia's mom. "Now, let's get Uncle Mort something in Tom's Sporting Goods. You know how much he likes baseball!"

Of course Lydia knew. That was one of the things he talked to Lydia about. He always wanted to teach her how to play it, but he also wanted to play it for his job in the major leagues. He told Lydia all about his dream.

They went into Tom's and made their way over to the baseball section, passing two men fighting over a football signed by some famous quarterback and a kid crying because his dad wouldn't buy him a trampoline.

Lydia looked up and saw a sign that said, "Sold Out." Next to the sign was a picture of a metal baseball bat tied with a big, silky, crimson bow.

"That would have been perfect," Lydia groaned into the empty rack where the bats used to be. This was the person she <u>most</u> wanted to give to at the holidays!

Suddenly, a small, blond girl walked up to Lydia and placed a metal bat in her hand, the same one as in the picture.

"You can have it," she said, quiet as a mouse.

She walked away so quickly that Lydia couldn't make out who it was, but she sort of looked like Kit.

"Mom, I got a gift for him!" cried Lydia, startling her mom who was looking at some tennis rackets.

"Oh, Lydia, that would be perfect! How in the world did you get it without someone stealing it from you?" asked Lydia's mom.

Lydia just shrugged. "So, who should we get gifts for next?" she asked, avoiding the question.

"Oh, I don't think we'll be as lucky to get any more gifts. It's getting later in the day and the Clifton Mall's becoming a madhouse. I don't want to risk getting in another one of those squabbles over a gift. We picked a bad day to shop."

The girls bought the baseball bat, and the cashier tied it with one of those crimson bows that was in the picture.

At least they had made a little progress on their shopping.

"I think I'll be making a lot of cards now that we don't have gifts, right?" asked Lydia, frowning as she got into the car.

"Right," said Mrs. Lips, driving out of the insanely full, Black Friday mall parking lot.

The holidays were coming up, and it seemed like they would be very interesting!

Chapter 8
Happy Holidays-At Least it Better Be Happy

Dear Diary,

Today we're having our big holiday celebration at my house, and I have a whole week of school off! Yes, I didn't say Christmas celebration or Chanukah celebration... my family celebrates both holidays. I celebrate Chanukah, because my mom and dad are Jewish, but my dad's brother (not Uncle Mort, that's my mom's brother), converted to Christianity. All of my little cousins, Lucy, Joseph, Hailey and Mimi, (Uncle Mort doesn't have any kids and he's not even married) celebrate Christmas. Today is not only Christmas, but also the 8th and last day of Chanukah. Our Chanukiah will be fully lit, and I'll finally get my Chanukah present. Usually, I'd get one each night, but this year the present must be so big that it's all my parents could get.

I want a lot of big things, so I'm really wondering what it is! We're going to have a huge dinner, play games, sing songs, and finally exchange presents. I can't wait to find out what I got. Whatever it is, I hope Judy gets something much worse!

> *Yours truly,*
> *Lydia Lips*

P.S. My gift to you is this drawing right here...

Do you like it?!

It felt like forever before five o'clock because Lydia was so anxious to find out what her gift was. The house was decorated merrily with all different scented candles, paper lanterns, and confetti. There were pictures of dreidels, Chanukiahs, Christmas trees, and presents. The house was an enlightening mix of different cultures.

The once bland table in the dining room had been transformed into a delightful dinner array, with china plates and cups, a gold-colored tablecloth, and a bouquet of poinsettias and roses in a bright blue pottery vase.

Not only was the house fancy, but the Lips had also cleaned themselves up. Lydia's long, dirty blond hair was swept into an elegant bun, and she was wearing a puffy, pink dress that she thought looked like a big, awful cupcake.

Her mom's hair was let loose for a change, a big difference from her normal dressy bun for work. Lydia thought her mom's shiny brown hair looked beautiful, especially when she was also wearing a long, sweeping evening gown. Mrs. Lips was complimented by her husband, who had on a crisp black tuxedo, which he would only wear on special occasions.

Lydia knew by looking around the room and smelling her mother's apple and cinnamon scented candle that this night would be perfect.

"Ding, Dong!" The doorbell finally rang, and Lydia rushed up to the front door as fast as she could without ruining her prim and proper hairdo.

"Happy Chanukah, Lydia," said Uncle Charley as he let himself inside.

"Merry Christmas, Uncle Charley," said Lydia, grinning.

His kids, Lydia's little cousins, hugged their big cousin and went running through the house in a mass of childish chaos. Uncle Charley's wife stepped in next and kissed Lydia on her head.

"You look beautiful," she cooed, but she looked very lovely herself in a scarlet party dress that went just below her knees. She was holding a present and motioned for Lydia to put it by the fireplace and sit at the table with the rest of the family, except for her kids, who were still screaming and running around chaotically.

Before Lydia could even think about sitting down, the doorbell rang again. It was Lydia's grandparents on her mom's side, followed by her grandparents on her dad's side. They all ambushed Lydia to pinch her cheeks and tell her how much she'd grown, even though it had only been a month since they saw her on Thanksgiving.

The last ring of the night made Lydia rush to the door with glee, for she knew who the door would be opened to.

"Uncle Mort!" cried Lydia and ran up to hug him hard.

"Lyd, my girl, how much I've missed you is infinite! We <u>really</u> have to catch up with each other!"

he said, breaking the hold on their hug, just to smile down into Lydia's face.

He dropped his presents by the fireplace and went to sit next to Lydia at the end of the well-decorated table.

It took some work rounding up Lucy, Joseph, Hailey, and Mimi, but soon, everyone was at the table, ready for a holiday meal.

"I'm so glad we could all be here today as a family," began Lydia's dad, sitting at the head of the table. "We're here to celebrate different holidays, but in all, we're celebrating joy, miracles, happiness, and love. I really hope you enjoy this meal we're about to have, but don't just enjoy the food, enjoy the happiness, and talk with each other. We're a family, and we will never forget this night!"

Mr. Lips got up from the table to get the food from the kitchen, all vegetarian in honor of Lydia. Lydia knew her <u>family</u> didn't care if she was vegetarian or not, unlike <u>some</u> people.

Uncle Mort did as Mr. Lips said and started to talk with Lydia.

"You know that baseball job I really wanted?" he asked.

"Of course, I would never forget! The one in the major leagues, right? It's major!" said Lydia, shaking away her thoughts of the delicious vegetarian food.

"I'm going to the tryouts in February! I'm really, really excited, and I thought I might teach you a little about baseball, so you can understand how awesome it would be if I got the job."

Lydia sighed, even though she loved being talked to. "You already taught me <u>so much</u> about baseball! Can't I have a break?!" she demanded.

"Oh, fine. I'll put baseball off for a little while, but I want to at least ask you a question. My dream is to play in the major leagues. What's your dream?" Uncle Mort asked patiently.

Lydia had to think for a moment. She wasn't so good when someone <u>else</u> was the one asking the question, because she wasn't usually put in that position.

Finally, she got the courage to answer. "My dream is to have a best friend that I can rely on ... one that can be ... forever."

"Don't you have a best friend? Isn't your best friend that girl you always talk about named Judy? Haven't you been friends with her forever?" he asked, baffled.

Lydia decided not to answer those questions. She had already answered one too many and decided to stay silent for the rest of dinner, even when she was eating her mom's famous latkes, so crispy and golden that it made you want to ask someone if any food could ever be better.

Finally, after indulging the huge holiday feast, the family was ready to exchange and receive presents by the fire.

"Eeeee!" squealed Lucy, the youngest cousin, excited about the presents.

Lydia felt just as excited, probably more so, about the one present she was getting. She chewed her finger nails as everyone else got their presents: Sweaters, Blanket Pets, toy trains, scented candles, candy canes, and a baseball bat that made a certain uncle especially happy. Everyone was also very happy with Lydia's cards.

Nobody had gotten Lydia anything yet. They must have thought she was too old for toys but too young for scented candles and purses. At least her parents got her a present, one which she'd be opening right now!

Mr. Lips shuffled through the pile of wrapping paper until he found one more gift to give. It was small, thin, and rectangular, a boring combination.

"This gift is for you, Lydia, and it's something I know you really want. Everyone here chipped in to get it for you, so what are you waiting for? Open it up!"

Lydia slowly tore away the paper dotted with snowmen to find an envelope.

What could be in an envelope so expensive that it had to be her only gift, paid for by her entire family?

Inside the envelope were four little rectangles. They each had a picture of two witches, one ugly and one pink and beautiful.

Written above the picture was the word, "Wicked", and below that was, "Front row seat".

Lydia was speechless, not out of happiness for her gift but of anger.

"Lydia, I knew you'd be in awe! I know how much you wanted tickets for the Broadway production, Wicked! It's for your birthday, February 27th! And there's a ticket for myself, your mom, you, and Judy, too! Now everyone's happy!" exclaimed Lydia's dad, ecstatically.

Lydia was definitely not happy. She remembered how, a couple of months ago, she wanted to see Wicked with Judy. Now, she wasn't friends with Judy, so her whole family had wasted <u>loads</u> of money for a ticket destined to go unused.

It was <u>supposed</u> to be for Lydia's friend, but Lydia had no friend. Lydia would never have a friend.

In a whisper, she said, "Thank you."

After that, everyone left.

Chapter 9
Skating

Dear Diary,

The rest of vacation since the party has been pretty boring. I've been watching T.V. and pretending to be drawing something. That something was supposed to be my perfect best friend, but it never ended up that way, so all of them ended up in the trash. Anyway, to get me out of the house and exercising, my mom signed me up for ice skating lessons at the Kennedy Memorial Rink at Kennedy Memorial High School, where I'll be going someday not that far away. I've never ice skated before, and I'm pretty nervous. Yesterday, my mom brought me to a skate store where I was fitted for my ice skates. They're white and squeeze my toes, but I don't care as long as I don't fall down in them. That's the thing about skating; even the professionals fall down. I don't care, though. I just care that I'll finally be getting off of the couch and getting some exercise besides gym class with Judy. Wish me luck!

Yours truly,
Lydia Lips

"Lydia, I have your skates, so please put on a sweatshirt and get in the car now," said Lydia's mom, who always liked being early for things.

Lydia went into her room to pick out a light blue sweatshirt, and then she hurried into the car as she was told.

After a short drive on the highway, Lydia's mom pulled into the parking lot of Kennedy Memorial High School. The rink, in a big building next to the school, was bright yellow, and above the door was a painting of a fierce komodo dragon with a hockey stick in its hand. That's the mascot of the Kennedy Komodo Dragons, Lydia discovered, as she read the caption under the picture: *Kennedy*

Are Questions that Bad?

Memorial Rink, Home of Kent, the Killer Komodo Dragon, and the Kennedy Komodo Dragons!

Lydia blew into her hands, which were frozen and numb from the winter air. Her mom just <u>had</u> to pick a freezing sport for her to do in the coldest time of the year!

They walked into the building where young girls were busily tying their skates and playing on the game machines available to kids at the rink.

A woman was also tying her skates on the blue bench.

"Ooo! That must be your teacher. Go over to her and say 'Hi'!" whispered Mrs. Lips.

Lydia slowly walked over to the bench. Her teacher wasn't the only person she spotted. She also saw a small, blond girl, quietly putting on her skates. That was Kit! Ice skating seemed perfect for Kit, so quiet and dainty!

"You must be Karen! I'm going to be your ice skating teacher. My name is Mrs. Wells. I'm pleased to have you as my student!" said Mrs. Wells, holding out her hand to shake with Lydia.

"Um, my name's Lydia," said Lydia, shaking Mrs. Wells's hand, forgiving her of the mistake.

Lydia bumbled over the many laces on her shiny new skates, finishing just as the door to the rink opened. She watched the whirring Zamboni and felt the intense chill of the icy room on her face. Other girls her age stampeded past her and glided onto the ice, moving towards the middle of the rink where the lesson would start.

Even Kit, with her shabby off-white skates, slowly moved across the ice.

Lydia just stood in the doorway of the rink. She had never skated before, and the ice looked so sharp — so cold and sharp and scary.

Mrs. Wells walked up to Lydia and startled her when she slipped her hand into hers.

"Put one foot in front of the other, Lydia. Lean on me, and we'll get across the ice smoothly. Just follow my lead!" she whispered.

Stumbling a little, Lydia, with her weight on Mrs. Wells, made it across the ice by putting one foot in front of the other. It didn't seem like the gliding some of the other girls did, but all in all, being on the ice made Lydia feel good, and she supposed it was more functional than watching television.

"Okay, class, welcome to the Kennedy Memorial Rink! If you didn't know, I'm Mrs. Wells, your teacher." She did a little spin on the ice, receiving some oos and aahs from the girls. "The first thing you need to know in order to skate is how to fall down."

Some of the girls looked worried that they were going to get hurt. Lydia empathized.

"All you have to do is bend down and fall on your bottom where you will be cushioned," continued Mrs. Wells.

Some of the girls giggled.

"This will help you in the future so nobody hurts themselves."

Everyone practiced falling down the right way. Lydia was surprised at how easy it was.

"Very good, Lydia," complimented Mrs. Wells.

After they did more practicing falling down, the teacher taught how to do swivels.

"Make your feet into a V shape and push them out and then in to make a lemon shape on the ice. Do those down and back, girls!"

Lydia made a small V with her feet and pushed as hard as she could, almost falling over but catching her balance. Mrs. Wells came over to show her how to do it right, and after that, everyone, including Lydia, was making numerous lemons all over the ice rink.

When everyone was done, they learned how to slowly glide and stop by using a snow plow.

"Whoosh!" went Lydia's skates, as she made a fluffy pile of snow from doing a perfect snow plow.

"Nicely done, Lydia! I can't believe that you've never skated before! You're a natural!" said Mrs. Wells, making Lydia blush.

"Okay class! Everyone has done very well today! You may free skate until the next group comes in!"

Lydia took her free skating time to practice her swivels, which sometimes looked like tiny kumquats rather large, juicy lemons. This skating thing wasn't actually as hard as she thought! It was also pretty fun, and it took her mind off of having no best friend to go to Wicked with. That would all melt away like ice- get it?

Lydia took her time skating back to the entrance. Her nose was red and sniffly and her hands were dry and numb, but she was truly happy.

"So, how was ice skating?" asked Mrs. Lips, taking off her daughter's skates and leading her to the car.

"Awesome, mom...skating is awesome," replied Lydia, hugging her bright white skates and touching the piece of snow still stuck to the blade from her perfect snow plow.

Chapter 10
A Fall in Winter

Dear Diary,

I absolutely <u>love</u> ice skating! The days have passed so quickly since my last lesson, and I have so much to tell you about it! My teacher's name is Mrs. Wells, and the only person I know in the class is Kit, whom nobody pays attention to anyway. That doesn't matter, because I'm an ice skating whiz! I don't mean to brag, Diary, but I've even mastered my swivels, which I practiced in our slippery entrance hall. Ice skating and me were meant for each other. We stick like glue! I love it! I also have a plan. Since I'm so good at skating, during free skating time, I'm going to skate really fast around the *room and impress everyone! Great plan, right? Diary, you should really try ice skating some time!*

Yours truly,
Lydia Lips

Lydia soon found herself going to school again. Winter break had zoomed by. She also found herself putting on her skates again after school for her second ice skating lesson. She'd been waiting for it all week, ever since her first lesson ended.

The lesson went by smoothly and quickly, just practicing the things they had learned last lesson. Lydia was even complimented on her perfect swivels!

As she had wanted, free skating time came. She was ready to impress everyone; maybe Mrs. Wells would be so impressed that she'd bump Lydia up to a higher level!

Lydia pushed her blade behind her and found herself gliding across the ice. She alternated feet and pushed herself to the limit to impress her teacher.

It felt so good and free to be skating with such skill. It was like heaven on earth!

A chilly wind swept through Lydia's hair as she glided by Mrs. Wells. This was her time to really impress!

She picked up speed, gliding faster now, the wind whipping against her cheeks. It was difficult though, and she wobbled a bit but managed to still keep her balance while cutting through the ice, now seeming less scary.

Lydia was about to come back around to her teacher, so she pushed harder, picking up more speed and gliding past her with ease.

Looking back and smiling at Mrs. Wells, Lydia's toe pick got caught in the ice and gave her an abrupt stop, thrusting her forward onto the ice.

She threw her arms over her face, her life flashing before her eyes. The ice was getting closer and closer, much too close for comfort. The rest, for Lydia, went black.

None of the other girls seemed to notice her fall, but Kit shrieked in horror.

"Aieeee! Lydia's hurt! She's fallen down and could be dead!" Kit cried, not as quietly as she usually was. Actually, she wasn't quiet at all.

Kit and Mrs. Wells rushed over to Lydia.

"My baby!" screamed Mrs. Lips, spotting her daughter idle on the icy ground.

"Is she alive?" asked Kit, placing her hand on Lydia's skate.

Mrs. Wells worriedly felt Lydia's heart. "This <u>never</u> happened at the old rink," she muttered to herself.

"Well?" asked Kit, desperately impatient.

"Yes, she's alive...just unconscious, and her arm is bleeding badly. We have to get her to the emergency room fast. She can get hypothermia if we don't act quickly," said Mrs. Wells, grateful and sad at the same time.

By now, most of the other girls had crowded around Lydia, loving this juicy and scary gossip. They couldn't wait to tell their friends that a girl fainted and almost died in their quiet ice skating class.

Mrs. Wells shot her hand into her pocket, pulled out her cell phone, and dialed three very important numbers.

Kit prayed that Lydia would be okay and shuddered at the gushing blood, coloring the ice from Lydia's arm.

In just a few minutes, men had come with a stretcher for Lydia, but they had no skates, and couldn't get onto the ice!

Everyone panicked frantically. A girl was stranded unconscious on the ice, and no one could come and get her!

"Wait, we can all push her to the entrance!" Kit exclaimed, happy with her idea to save Lydia.

The girls and Mrs. Wells all skated slowly while kneeling down to push Lydia across the ice. It was hard work, kneeling for so long, and pushing Lydia at the same time, but finally, they were at the entrance of the rink where the men put Lydia gently onto the stretcher.

Back on the rink, a line of blood stained the ice where Lydia was dragged.

Mrs. Lips kissed her daughter's head and asked if she could come with her to the emergency room.

"May I come too?" asked Kit to one of the men.

Making them each smile, they were allowed to come, but the ride to the hospital was gloomy. More blood was coming from Lydia's arm, and she hadn't woken up yet.

Soon, Lydia was in a warm bed, with her arm still bleeding and needing to be tended to.

A woman dressed in a pristine white robe walked into the hospital room. Mrs. Lips jumped up to meet her.

"Will she be okay?" she moaned, as Kit tried to wipe up some of the blood protruding onto the bed with her sleeve.

"The doctor will be in shortly to give her extra blood. I'll also need to take an x-ray because that arm isn't looking very good, but I'm sure she'll be fine!" said the nurse, her smile looking more like an uncomfortable frown.

Mrs. Lips tried to hide her tears as she gently kissed her unconscious daughter's head.

The nurse led her and Kit out of the room when the doctor arrived. He had a <u>very</u> crucial and important job to do!

If Lydia were awake, she'd have been asking <u>many</u> questions.

Chapter 11
The Benefits and Doubts of an X-Ray

Dear Diary,

My mom brought you here so I could have something to do while I was waiting. You might ask where I am, and what I am waiting for. Well, I'm in the hospital, don't ask, I don't know why either, and I'm waiting for the doctor to tell me the results of my x-ray. I can tell it won't be good because I'm in excruciating pain right now, and there's a needle attached to my other arm to give me more blood. By the color of the bed, I think I lost a lot. I'm a little dizzy right now, and it's getting hard to write with my arm *all wrapped up in bandages and a cast. I think I'm going to take a nap...*

"Lydia! Lydia, wake up!" cried Mrs. Lips.

Lydia opened one eye halfway, spotting an empty pack of blood attached to her catheter.

The doctor walked by with a paper in his hand, probably the highly-anticipated x-ray results.

At that point, Lydia had opened both eyes but was still a bit groggy.

"Doctor, tell me the news! Is she okay?" yelled Lydia's mom, frantic again.

The doctor ignored her and went over to Lydia, replacing the pack of blood for her, now just fluids to keep her awake.

He stroked her head and whispered something in her ear.

"What?!" yelled Lydia at the top of her lungs. She was surprised at her own loudness.

Just outside the room, Kit jumped in surprise.

"Wait, did I just see Kit?" asked Lydia, changing the topic out of her own confusion.

"Yeah," said Kit, quietly walking into the hospital room, disobeying the doctor's orders to give Lydia some space to recover.

"Kit, why in the world are <u>you</u> here?" asked Lydia, looking up at the little blond girl.

Kit just looked down at Lydia and grinned sympathetically.

"She saved you," Lydia's mom whispered to her daughter, who was in total shock.

Kit quietly shrugged, not taking the credit.

"When you fell on the ice, Kit was the one who warned everyone, and she was the first one to want to help you, honey. I saw it all," said Mrs. Lips, grinning. "She also wanted to come on the ambulance with you. She wanted to make sure you were okay."

Lydia stayed quiet until she finally opened her mouth again.

"Kit, were you the one who gave me the last baseball bat in the store?" whispered Lydia.

"Yeah," quietly answered Kit, still smiling.

"I was just wondering, Kit … why are you so … so nice? You're never mean to anyone, you're always quiet, and you always want to help. None of my friends are like that. None of my friends are…" Lydia paused to think for a moment until she finished her statement, "…friends."

Everyone was quiet for a moment, even the doctor who had heard it all and was still in the room. It was like mourning someone's death, or rather quietly celebrating a birth.

It was broken by a few words from Lydia. "Kit, do you want to be friends?" she asked.

Kit nodded in her quiet way.

"But wait," Mrs. Lips broke up the happy moment. "Lydia, why did you scream before? What did the doctor tell you? Are you okay, sweetie?" she asked frantically.

"Don't worry," said the doctor, twirling his stethoscope in his fingers. "Lydia just has..."

Lydia spun around to face the other way in her bed as to not hear the bad news again.

"...a broken arm," he said.

Chapter 12
On Broadway!

Dear Diary,

Time has really flown, and I've done so much in the past few months. A lot of that has been having play dates with my new best friend, Kit. My arm is healing nicely, too! I barely realized that my birthday was coming up, but now I see that it's today! My parents already gave me a present, a laptop! It's _so_ cool, and I know it'll be great for typing up things for school. Today is not only my birthday, but it's also the day I have tickets to see *Wicked* on Broadway. When I got the tickets, I was angry because there was an extra ticket to bring Judy, and I was mad at her. I'm still mad at her, but I've decided to ask

Kit to come with me. I really hope she can come!
Wish me a happy birthday!

Yours truly,
  Lydia Lips

"Ring, Ring!" went the phone as Lydia finished dialing Kit's number, a number she had called so much that she could dial it without even thinking.

"Hey, Lydia," said Kit.

"Kit, you know I was wondering..." started Lydia.

"Wondering what? Wondering if I got you a present? Well, of course I did! I didn't forget your birthday!" exclaimed Kit.

It seemed that ever since becoming best friends with Lydia, Kit had gotten more confident and even a little bit louder.

"No, no, it's not that, I'm not even expecting a present actually. I was just hoping that you can come somewhere with me..."

Lydia didn't even finish her sentence before Kit jumped in and said, "Oh, of course I'm free! My parents will let me go wherever you want me to go!"

Lydia grinned, even though Kit couldn't see that through the telephone line. She could hear the happiness in her response, though.

"That's great! My parents got me tickets to Wicked for Chanukah, and I get to pick a friend to come with me. Of course it's you! Tell your parents to drive you to my house at 1:30. My parents will take us to the show!"

She hung up, not like the time with Judy. That time she hung up out of rage, of sheer madness with a mix of sadness and spite. This time she hung up because she had said what she wanted, and she needed time to pick out the outfit she was going to wear for the best day of her life!

Time passed quickly since the morning, and Lydia had decided to wear a cropped jacket with velvety pants, an outfit that made her feel good. 1:30 neared and Lydia's mom called out, "Judy's here. A car came into the driveway."

"Mom, you know I'm not friends with Judy anymore! I invited Kit to see the show!" said Lydia, annoyed that her mom didn't remember what had happened.

"Oh, I knew that," sighed Mrs. Lips, but her daughter was already out the door.

"Lydia!" Kit cried when she came to her, the car driving back down the street. "I couldn't resist giving you a present," she said, wrapping a silver chain around Lydia's neck.

Kit had one too, half of a smiley face with the word 'Best' engraved on it. She could already tell that hers said 'Friends'.

"Do you like it?" Kit asked, holding her own necklace in her fingertips.

Lydia just nodded and smiled, as they got into Mr. Lips's car. They were on their way to New York City, clutching tickets to a Broadway musical.

The play turned out to be amazing, with elaborate dances, songs, and costumes. Kit said that the spin on "The Wizard of Oz" was much better than the real thing. And it was true. The woman playing Glinda had such a wonderful, high voice and was <u>such</u> a great actress! Her pink, puffy, costumes didn't hurt either. Elphaba wasn't too bad herself, but Lydia and Kit agreed that the last song was the best part of the play.

It was called "For Good", and it told a lot about friendship, how it comes and goes, but always leaves an impact.

The last line of the song was the best, "Because I knew you, I have been changed for good".

When Lydia was friends with Judy, all she got out of it was trickery and sadness. Judy was mean to her, not a good friend at all, and Lydia never wanted to see her again.

But Kit on the other hand was a good person, a good friend. From her, Lydia had learned that giving is great, and both kindness and caring are important in a friendship. Lydia had really been changed "for good" because of Kit. Lydia had been changed for good.

Chapter 13
Dear Diary

Dear Diary,

As you know, a lot has happened to me in the past year, to my friends, family, and how I think. There have been some bad things, like when I broke my arm. It's all better now, though. Another bad thing has been my relationship with Judy, that's all over too, and I don't regret it. She isn't the kind of person that a friend should be like. It's not as if there haven't been good things, too, Diary. My mom came back from Amsterdam, and we're a family again. Also, my Uncle Mort's dream came true to be a baseball player in the major leagues. I remember the day he told me his dream. He stopped talking about baseball to ask me what my dream was. I said it was to have a best friend I could rely on forever, but there was a problem then. I didn't know what a friend was. With Judy, I thought I had a friend, but I didn't. Judy tricked me and I tricked her, all because of one of my questions. I wondered if questions were that bad, but it wasn't the question that was bad, it was the friend. When I met Kit, I knew she was quiet, I knew she was nice, I knew she was okay, but I didn't know she was a friend. It's not until you get to know a person that you get to know if they're a friend...or rather not, like Judy. If a person can't accept who you are and can't be compassionate, they're not a friend. Kit is, and I suppose you are, too, Diary. When I got you, you were my only friend. You let me talk to you, and write in you, and that was about it. Sometimes that's all you need in a friend, someone you can talk to, but most of all, someone who will listen to you. Sometimes you need more, like someone who will talk back, but as long as they're nice, they're a friend. I knew I was wrong before. I knew Judy couldn't be a friend, but, I wanted her to be, and that's why I blamed our friendship on questions, but questions are off the hook now. I guess questions aren't so bad after all.

Yours truly,
    Lydia Lips

The End

About the Author...Hannah Rappaport

Hannah lives with her family including her hermit crab, Dizzy, in Orange, CT. She enjoys singing, drawing, swimming, and of course, writing. Being an eleven year old, she has lots of friends at her school, and friend problems, too, but she's happy to say that she knows what a true friend is, just like Lydia had learned. Just like Lydia, she's a young vegetarian because of her immense love for animals, which is why she made her website, GVOAHN.com. Her dad is an author, too; go <u>Legacy of Ogma</u>! She also loves that she can tell a message in her stories, which is the whole reason she writes!